Ignis

*For Ann, with love* ❖ G. W.

*For Barbara* ❖ P. J. L.

Text copyright © 2001 by Gina Wilson
Illustrations copyright © 2001 by P.J. Lynch

First U.S. edition 2001

Library of Congress Cataloging-in-Publication Data
Wilson, Gina.
Ignis / written by Gina Wilson ; illustrated by P.J. Lynch
—1st U.S. ed.
p.  cm.
Summary: Though he is admired by others, a young dragon
does not feel complete because he cannot breathe fire.
ISBN 0-7636-1623-0
[1. Dragons—Fiction. 2. Identity—Fiction.]
I. Lynch, Patrick James, ill. II. Title.
PZ7.W6946 Ij 2001
[E]—dc21    2001025219

10 9 8 7 6 5 4 3 2 1

Printed in Italy

This book was typeset in Slimbach Medium.
The illustrations were done in watercolor and gouache.

Candlewick Press
2067 Massachusetts Avenue
Cambridge, Massachusetts 02140

visit us at www.candlewick.com

# IGNIS

Gina Wilson

illustrated by
# P.J. Lynch

CANDLEWICK PRESS
CAMBRIDGE, MASSACHUSETTS

**I**GNIS lived with his sister, Flamma, and Grandragon. They had their own warm, dark cave in Dragonland, which is a secret place no bigger than a village, hidden in rocks at the foot of a steep mountain.

Ignis had fiery red scales, flaring nostrils, and a spiky tail. His wings, depending on the weather, opened like silk umbrellas or gossamer parasols.

His friends all admired him very much. Some even wished they were him, instead of themselves. He could run the fastest and fly the highest.

❖But Ignis was sad.

Every night, he sat at the back of the cave, huffing and puffing till he thought he would burst, but not a single flame ever appeared, not a flicker.

Grandragon stirred her pot. "All in good time," she said. "Never worry."

"Come and light stars with me," said Flamma. "You might just get the hang of it without thinking."

❖But Ignis wasn't comforted. He couldn't light stars, and he couldn't start the cave fire to boil the kettle. He couldn't play *Fling a Flame* or *All Blaze Together*. He could only watch.

His best friend, Scintilla, watched with him. She warmed him with her amber eyes. "I love you anyway."

"I love you too," said Ignis. "But it's no good unless I find my fire. I don't feel like a dragon at all. Maybe I'm really something else."

❖One dawn, Ignis set off into the thick forest that ran all the way around the foot of the mountain.

In the river he spotted Poto, floating along with just his eyes showing. "Hello," said Poto oozily. "Come on in, if you like."

So Ignis spent the morning slowly flowing with the current, and the afternoon caking his scales with mud. But by evening he knew he wasn't a hippo. His mouth was much too small and he was worried the water might rust his scales.

"You're a wonderful friend," he told Poto, "but I'll have to be on my way. I'm not really a hippo, you know."

Poto laughed. "I can see that, Little Puff of Smoke! You're a dragon!"

"But where's my fire?" said Ignis.

"Inside," said Poto. "Best place when you're swimming."

Ignis waved goodbye. "I won't forget you," he called, and felt a friendly lick of flame flaring inside his chest. He gave a cough, and then another, but it wouldn't come out.

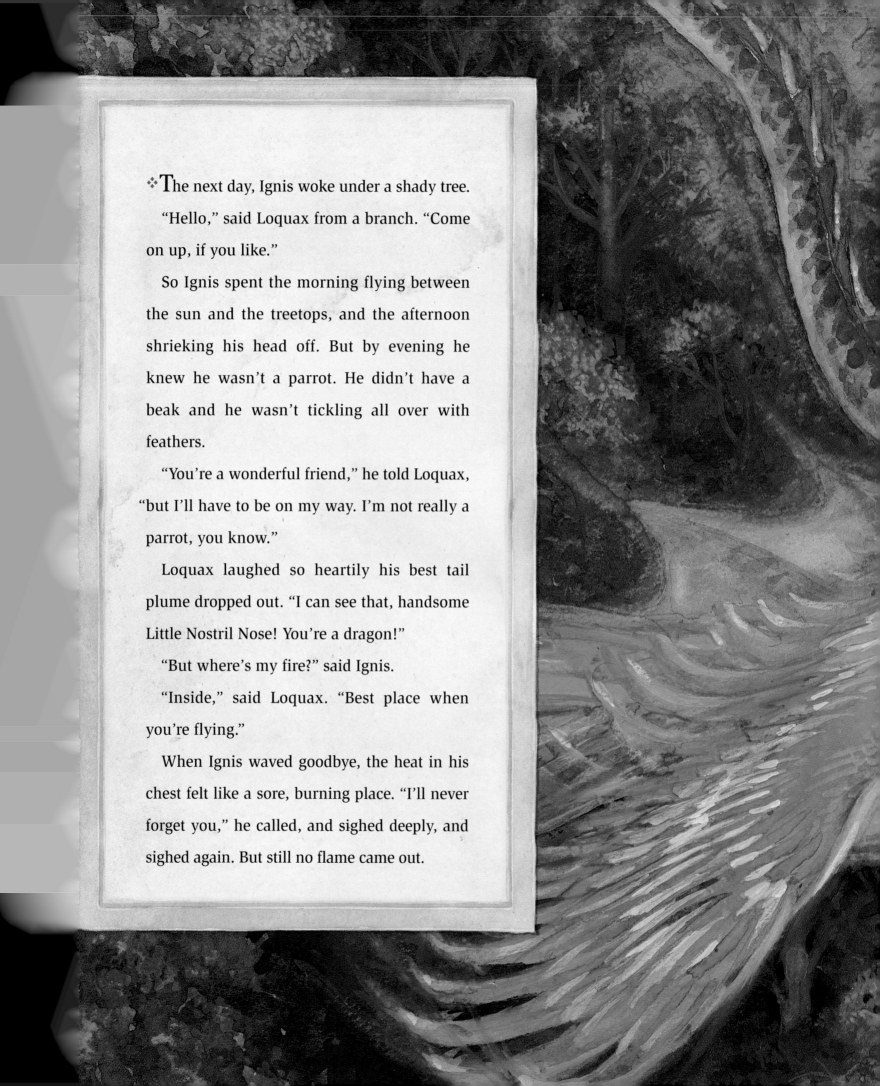

❖The next day, Ignis woke under a shady tree.

"Hello," said Loquax from a branch. "Come on up, if you like."

So Ignis spent the morning flying between the sun and the treetops, and the afternoon shrieking his head off. But by evening he knew he wasn't a parrot. He didn't have a beak and he wasn't tickling all over with feathers.

"You're a wonderful friend," he told Loquax, "but I'll have to be on my way. I'm not really a parrot, you know."

Loquax laughed so heartily his best tail plume dropped out. "I can see that, handsome Little Nostril Nose! You're a dragon!"

"But where's my fire?" said Ignis.

"Inside," said Loquax. "Best place when you're flying."

When Ignis waved goodbye, the heat in his chest felt like a sore, burning place. "I'll never forget you," he called, and sighed deeply, and sighed again. But still no flame came out.

❖The next morning, Ignis woke on the very farthest side of the mountain, as far from Dragonland as could be.

Cara was sitting there on a little locked gate, swinging her legs. "You must be a really real dragon!" she said.

"I might be," said Ignis. "But where's my fire?"

"Inside, with any luck," said Cara. "We don't want you setting these trees alight. This gate's bolted to keep out forest monsters while I'm staying with my gran. But you can fly over it, if you want to."

"Maybe *I'm* a monster," said Ignis.

"No," said Cara. "You're beautiful."

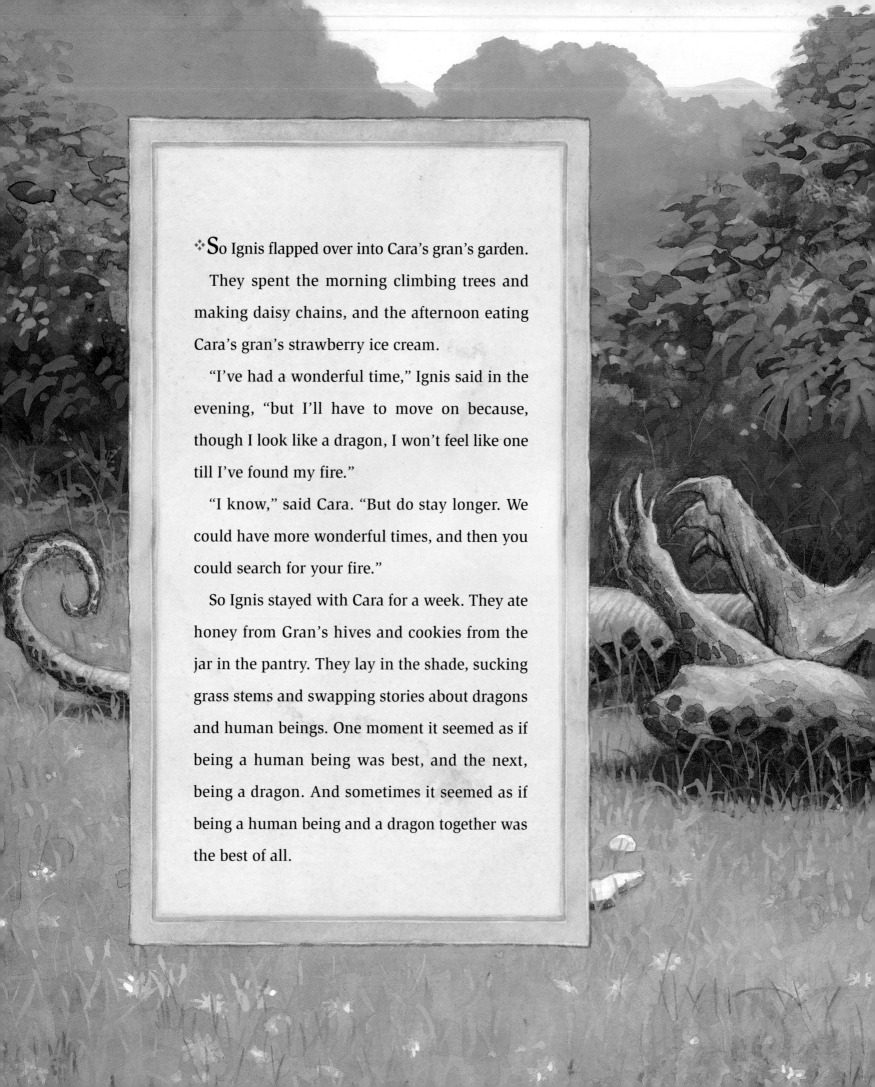

❖So Ignis flapped over into Cara's gran's garden.

They spent the morning climbing trees and making daisy chains, and the afternoon eating Cara's gran's strawberry ice cream.

"I've had a wonderful time," Ignis said in the evening, "but I'll have to move on because, though I look like a dragon, I won't feel like one till I've found my fire."

"I know," said Cara. "But do stay longer. We could have more wonderful times, and then you could search for your fire."

So Ignis stayed with Cara for a week. They ate honey from Gran's hives and cookies from the jar in the pantry. They lay in the shade, sucking grass stems and swapping stories about dragons and human beings. One moment it seemed as if being a human being was best, and the next, being a dragon. And sometimes it seemed as if being a human being and a dragon together was the best of all.

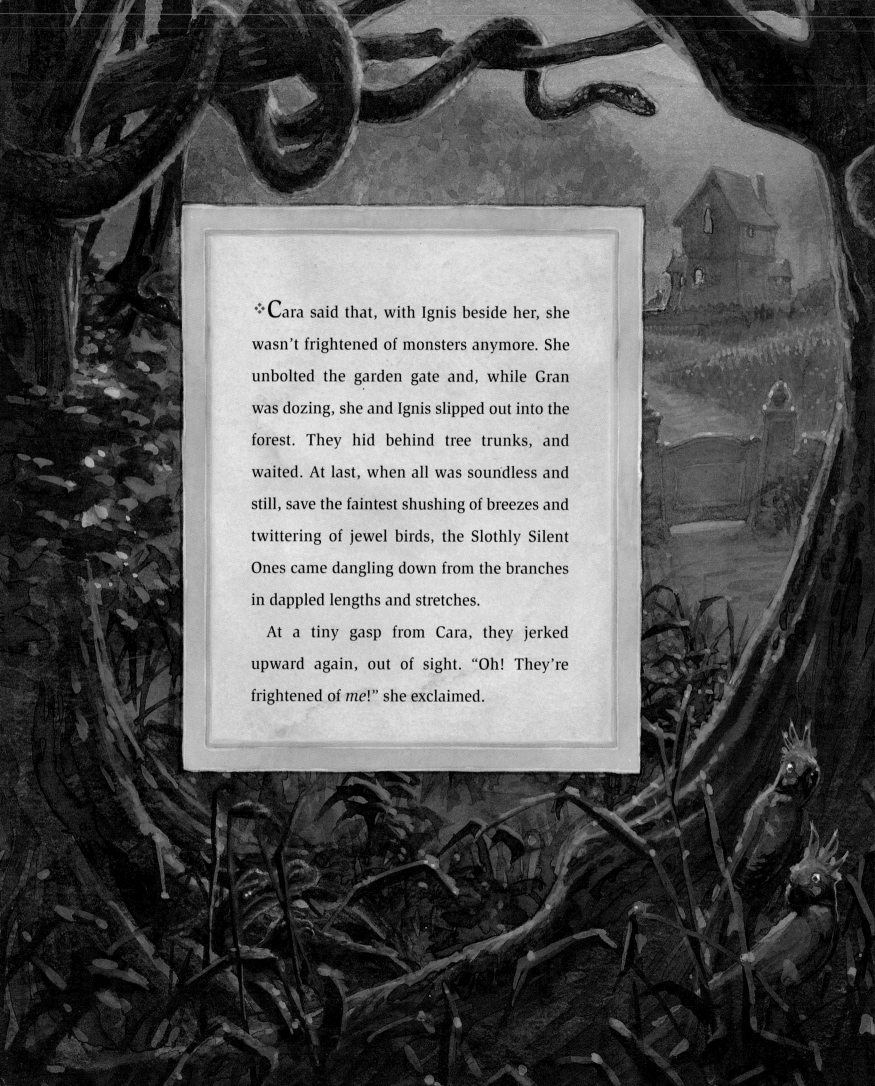

❖Cara said that, with Ignis beside her, she wasn't frightened of monsters anymore. She unbolted the garden gate and, while Gran was dozing, she and Ignis slipped out into the forest. They hid behind tree trunks, and waited. At last, when all was soundless and still, save the faintest shushing of breezes and twittering of jewel birds, the Slothly Silent Ones came dangling down from the branches in dappled lengths and stretches.

At a tiny gasp from Cara, they jerked upward again, out of sight. "Oh! They're frightened of *me*!" she exclaimed.

❖That night, Ignis flew Cara up past the stars, higher than he'd ever been before. They paddled in bubbling moonstreams. They sat on the dark shore and watched the almost invisible night gazelles stealing down to drink.

Back they glided to Gran's house, Cara fast asleep on Ignis's back, his wings curved to keep her from falling.

❖At the end of the week, they sat sadly, knowing it was time for goodbye.

"We've had lots of wonderful times," sighed Cara. "I knew we would. But I'm going home tomorrow. School starts on Monday. I can't wait to tell my best friend about you."

"I have a best friend too," said Ignis. "But I'm not going home till I've found my fire."

Cara kissed him. "For luck!" she whispered. "I know you'll find it. And then you'll go home. I can always imagine you playing there, with hundreds of other dragons!" She skipped away.

Ignis's heart felt fiery. "Remember me!" he shouted.

"Of course!" Cara shouted back. "This has been my Dragon Summer. You only get one."

❖Ignis sat in a heap. Beyond the gate, the forest looked dark and thick, and he was certain he'd never find anything else in it that was as good as what he'd found already. *This time, I'll climb to the top of the mountain,* he thought. *I haven't looked there.*

He panted up the track, feeling lonely and sad without Cara. His heart was still fiery, but his gasps wouldn't turn into flames.

Higher up, the mountain was icy and white. "I'd just melt all this in a couple of puffs," Ignis shivered, "if I were a *real* dragon."

He thought of Poto, the real hippo, and Loquax, the real parrot, and Cara, the real little girl, all happily playing with their friends, and he could feel a great burst of fire blazing away inside him. But it wouldn't come out. He slumped down and buried his head in his wings.

Then he pictured Scintilla, waiting to hear all about the forest and its inhabitants; and all about the mountain, and whatever might be waiting at the top.

"But I don't even know that myself!" he exclaimed. Up he jumped, and kept on climbing.

The top of the mountain was covered with silvery powder, like the ash of Grandragon's cave fire. It puffed up in glittering clouds. Above him, the highest peak of all shone in the sunset, orange and yellow and pink. *Like flame!* thought Ignis.

❖But when at last he arrived, there was only a deep, dark hole. *"Volcano,"* he whispered. He poked his head over the side. The hole was black as night. It was sooty and bottomless.

*"But its fire's gone out!"* He turned away. There was nothing here. All he wanted was the safe warm cave of home.

He covered his eyes and began to cry.

❖And at that moment, the very last spark from the volcano's very last eruption, one hundred years ago, came wandering out into the open, weak and wavering and looking for somewhere to light.